# The Hidden Forest

## by JEANNIE BAKER



Greenwillow Books, *An Imprint of* HarperCollins*Publishers*



I wish to acknowledge the support and assistance I have had from many people, in particular David Blackwell, Haydn Washington, Graham Edgar, Karen Gowlett-Holmes, Susan Griffiths, Gary Myors, Andrew Payne, Jaime Plaza Van Roon, Craig Sanderson, and Professor H. B. S. Womersley.

The collage-construction artwork was built with collected natural materials such as pressed seaweeds, sponges, and sands. The kelp was modeled with a translucent artist's clay, and the seawater with resin. The collages were then reproduced in full color from photographs by David Blackwell. The text type is Goudy Sans Medium.
 http://www.harperchildrens.com

Library of Congress Cataloging-in-Publication Data: Baker, Jeannie. The hidden forest / by Jeannie Baker. p. cm. "Greenwillow Books." Summary: When a friend helps him retrieve the fishtrap he lost while trying to fish just off the coast of eastern Tasmania, Ben comes to see the Giant Kelp forest where he lost his fishtrap in a new light. ISBN 0-688-15760-2 (trade). ISBN 0-688-15761-0 (lib. bdg.) [1. Giant kelp—Fiction. 2. Kelps—Fiction. 3. Tasmania—Fiction.] I. Title. PZ7.B1742Hi 2000 [E]—dc21 99-23175 CIP

1 2 3 4 5 6 7 8 9 10 First Edition

Down in the dark, tangled world of the weed,
there are big and small fish.
Ben knows they are there.
But time after time only minnows come up in his fish trap.
Ben empties them out in disgust
to let them die.
He wants something much bigger.

This time when he tries to raise the trap, it will not move.
Ben yanks at it with all his strength!

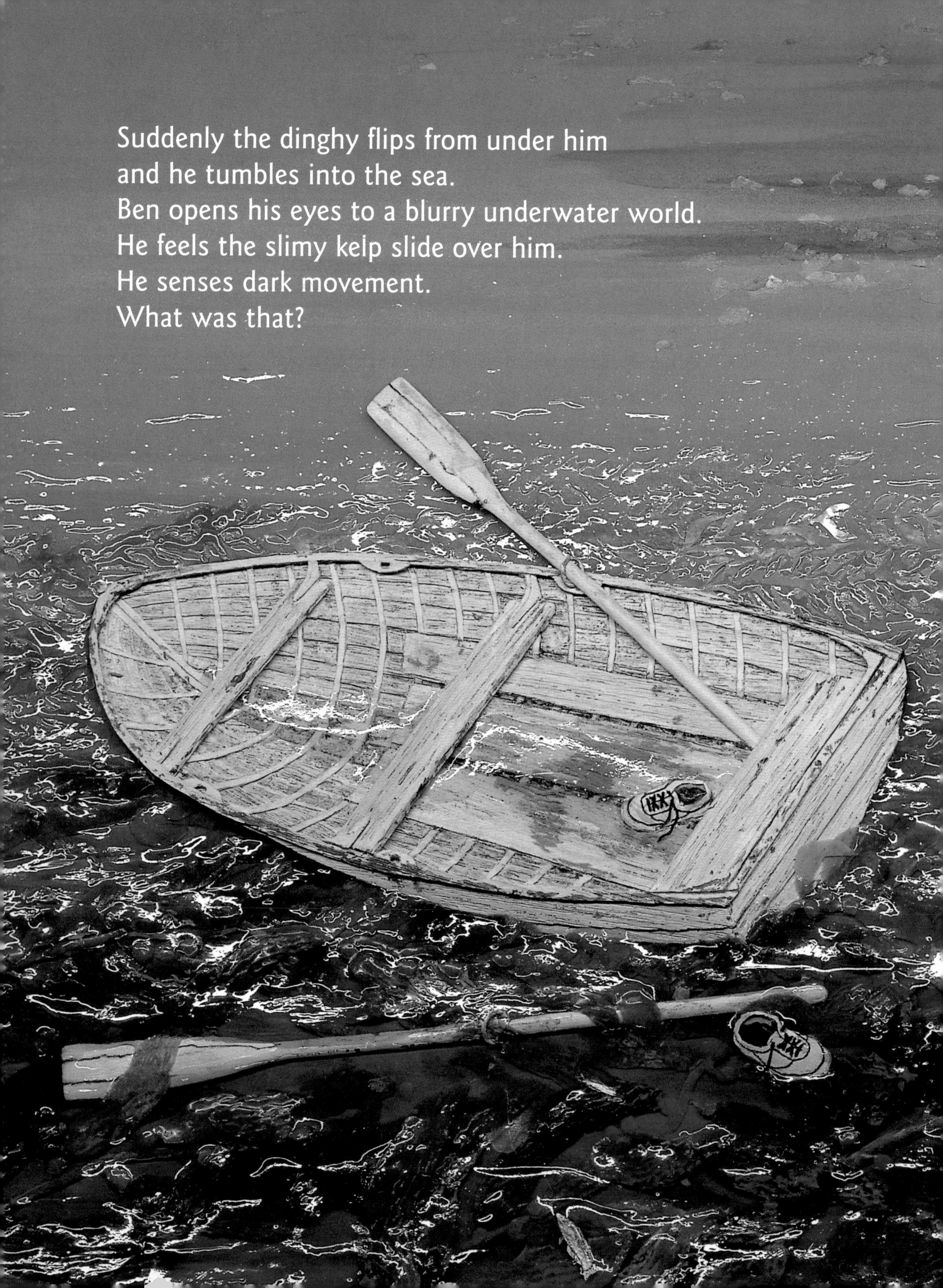

Suddenly the dinghy flips from under him
and he tumbles into the sea.
Ben opens his eyes to a blurry underwater world.
He feels the slimy kelp slide over him.
He senses dark movement.
What was that?

REAL
FRESH!
REAL
VALUE!

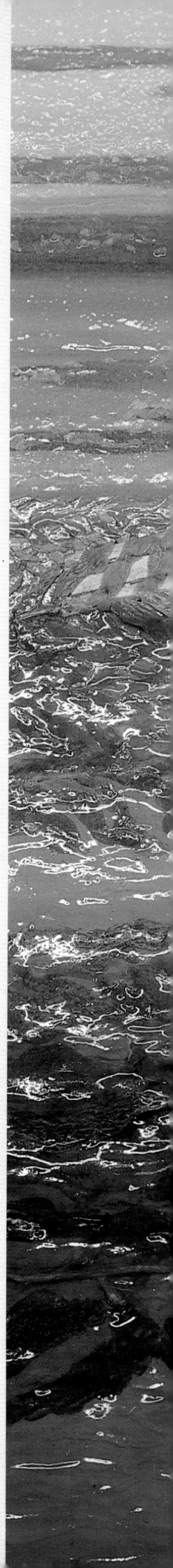

Ben panics.
He is afraid some unknown creature will grab his legs
as he scrambles back into the dinghy.
Did he see something, or was it his imagination?
The kelp clings to his oars and won't let him go.

Ben eventually rows free of the kelp and calms down. He must recover his trap, but he will need the help of a friend who can dive down to untangle it.

He thinks of Sophie.

Sophie is a strong diver.
She agrees to help if Ben will come with
her to see the world under the waves.

Ben gazes at the surface of the water,
but it's like a mirror.
He worries about what might be lurking below
and cautiously lowers himself into the sea.

To his surprise, Ben finds himself floating above a mysterious underwater forest that sways back and forth with the rolling of the waves.

Gigantic golden trees of kelp
reach toward the sun.
Shafts of sunlight
shimmer in their branches.

Ben waits anxiously
while Sophie untangles the trap.
At last it is free!

Sophie holds out her hand to Ben
and takes him to explore the different kelps
growing near the rocky shore.

Ben holds on to a piece of bull kelp and rides with it
as it sways and stretches with the tide.
When the kelp touches him,
it feels like velvet swirling against his skin.

He parts some kelp to reveal rock
alive with all kinds
of strangely beautiful textures.

Sophie shows Ben how he can hold
his breath and dive down into the forest
to look for seadragons.

Sensing a presence behind him,
Ben turns.

A whale, watching him closely, glides gently by.
Ben is overwhelmed with wonder.

Ben and Sophie catch glimpses of its dark, gleaming shape
rolling and sliding against the kelp
as it passes on around the bay.

Together they pull up the fish trap.
Ben gazes in fascination at his catch.

But Ben sees things differently now. . . .
He sees how wonderful these creatures are
here in their mysterious, hidden world.

He feels this is where they belong.

## AUTHOR'S NOTE

Kelp forests of various species grow in the shallow cold or temperate waters of both the northern and southern hemispheres, especially where there are rocky surfaces.

A kelp forest is structured in layers, with each layer representing a distinctive habitat for different plants and animals. Some forests are important nurseries for fish.

The main kelp shown in this book is known as Giant Kelp or String Kelp (*Macrocystis pyrifera*). This species is the fastest growing (in height) plant in the world and can grow 14 inches (35 cm) a day. Forests of Giant Kelp occur on the coldwater coasts of North and South America, South Africa, southeastern Australia, New Zealand, and the islands near Antarctica.

The kelp forest community here is based on one found on the east coast of Tasmania, where some scientists are concerned that Giant Kelp is disappearing.